D0190961

# Wizards
## OF WAVERLY PLACE
### THE MOVIE

# Wizards OF WAVERLY PLACE THE MOVIE

# The Junior Novel

Adapted by Alice Alfonsi

Executive Producer Peter Murrieta

Producer Kevin Lafferty

Director Lev L. Spiro

Written by Dan Berendsen

Based on the series created by Todd J. Greenwald

DISNEP PRESS

NEW YORK

Printed in the United States of America

First Edition
1 3 5 7 9 10 8 6 4 2

Library of Congress Control Number on file.
ISBN 978-1-4231-2474-0

For more Disney Press fun, visit www.disneybooks.com

Visit DisneyChannel.com

# CHAPTER 1

Alex Russo looked at the sign on the front door of the Waverly Sub Station, her family's sandwich shop in Greenwich Village. It read: CLOSED. ON VACATION!

First thing the next morning, her family was flying to the Caribbean, to the island where her parents had met and fallen in love. They wanted to relive their courtship, it seemed.

Alex smiled smugly to herself. Although her two brothers, Justin and Max, were going along, Alex had gotten permission to stay at

her best friend Harper Evans's house. Alex could hardly wait until the rest of her family hit the road!

After closing the blinds, Alex turned to face the empty restaurant. But it wasn't *totally* empty. She had just spotted Justin's messenger bag on the counter.

"How careless of Justin to leave his messenger bag around," she said aloud to herself. "I mean, who knows who might get into it, right?" Like me! she thought. After all, what self-respecting sister could resist a little snooping when it concerned her older brother?

"Oh, Justin. I found your bag," Alex called out—very softly. "Do you mind if I look at all your personal stuff?" She paused and waited for a response, which, naturally, didn't come. "Okay, thanks!"

Alex opened the bag—and her eyes widened in surprise. "No way!" She reached inside. But as soon as she touched the thin silver object, there was a flash of mystical light and—

"Let go!" Alex yelled suddenly.

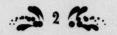

But whatever was holding on to her didn't listen. Instantly, Alex's hands were sucked inside the bag, followed by her arms, and then her shoulders! She squirmed as the bag continued trying to swallow her, knocking over all the chairs and tables around her.

"What's going on?" Alex's mother, Theresa Russo, cried as she rushed into the dining room.

Alex's dad, Jerry Russo, heard the commotion, too. He ran in from the kitchen, with Justin and Alex's younger brother, Max, behind him.

By then, only Alex's feet were showing.

"Hey, cool!" Max exclaimed. "Whatever it is, can we keep it?"

"I knew it," Justin said with a smirk. "Alex has been going through my bag, just as I thought she would. So I put a spell on it."

Mrs. Russo sighed. "Ah, yes, an enchanted messenger bag. How did we *ever* manage without one?" Then she rolled her eyes and walked out of the room.

Mr. Russo nodded to Justin, who shrugged

 3

and took out his magic wand. *"Magic was used to protect the bag. Reverse the spell and release the bag!"* Justin chanted.

With a bright burst of magical energy, Alex was freed.

"Okay, fine!" she cried, tossing back her long brown hair. "I was going through his stupid bag. But look what I found—" Alex held up the silver wand she'd discovered in Justin's bag, along with a small, ancient-looking book entitled *The Book of Forbidden Spells*.

"The family wand *and* a book of forbidden spells!" she told her dad. "He took it out of the lair without permission!" She glanced at her brother. "My respect for you is increasing," she added.

"Dad *gave* it to me," Justin informed her. "I would never take something without asking," he said.

Alex scowled and turned to her dad. "How could you give this to Justin? It's *forbidden*. I know because it's right there in the title. You said we weren't allowed to touch it. You said we weren't ready."

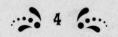

"And by *we*, I think he meant *you*," Justin told her.

"Alex," Mr. Russo explained, "if, when, *someday*, possibly, you pass or actually show up for any of your exams . . . you can use the spell book and the family wand, too. They're *extremely* powerful and take a certain level of responsibility that . . ."

"But I'm responsible!" Alex interrupted. "I *can* be trusted. It's unfair. To me . . . and to Max." She turned toward her little brother, who was also very interested in Justin's messenger bag.

Still, didn't Alex have a point? One day, they would have to hold a family wizard competition, and from then on, only one of them would be able to keep their magical powers. But in the meantime, they were *all* wizards in training and deserved an equal chance to develop their talents—as far as Alex was concerned.

Just then, Mrs. Russo returned with a broom and handed it to Alex. "I don't have an opinion about this great *wand* whoop-di-do," she said, "but I *do* know that if anybody should be playing nice right now, it's you."

Alex opened her mouth to try and defend herself.

"Don't push," her mother warned her. Then she nodded to her husband. "We need to go."

Justin stepped up next to Alex. "I'll take those," he said, motioning toward the wand and book. Alex picked up Justin's bag and dropped the wand inside.

"Here," she said, handing the bag back to her brother. "I don't even want them." Alex grinned slyly as Justin walked away. "Total lie," she whispered, glancing at the spell book she was still holding.

Then, she suddenly noticed her mother and father putting on their coats. "Hey, where's everybody going?" she asked.

Mrs. Russo, meanwhile, had begun to give her sons instructions. "I want you two done packing by the time we get back," she said. "Your father and I have a million errands to run before we leave tomorrow."

"This is going to be the greatest vacation ever!" Justin cheered.

"Are there going to be volcanoes?" Max asked.

"No," Justin said, rolling his eyes.

"Then how great can it be?" Max asked, disappointed.

Suddenly, the restaurant door opened and Alex's best friend Harper walked in.

"Hi, Mr. and Mrs. Russo," Harper said pleasantly.

"Hi, Harper," replied Mr. Russo. Then he turned to Alex. "What's Harper doing here?" he asked his daughter suspiciously.

"Oh, um, hey, I was thinking that since you're all getting ready for a trip that *I* don't have to go on . . ." Alex began.

"Don't push," Mrs. Russo told Alex again. "I already told you that you can't go to that party. It's all the way in Brooklyn, I don't know the girls' parents, and I don't want you out late."

"Mom, please," Alex begged. "*Everybody* is going to this party."

"That's true," Harper chimed in. "They handed out, like, a thousand flyers."

"You're destroying my *life*," Alex told her mom.

"Which is the same thing you said when I tried to 'force' you to go on vacation with us," Mrs. Russo said with a frown.

"Well, it worked then," Alex said with a shrug.

"Alex," her mother said, after taking a deep breath, "I know you're growing up, and you want some independence, and that you'll be fine at Harper's while we're gone. But you have to understand that leaving you behind is very hard for me. So just go easy, okay?"

"Okay," Alex said. She smiled and gave her mom a hug. Then she turned to her father and grinned. "Dad? Please? I'll just pop into the party and—"

Mrs. Russo groaned and threw up her hands.

"No," Mr. Russo replied firmly. "You heard your mother. And just so we're clear," he went on, "you may not walk, fly, teleport, or pop out of this building. Do you understand?" He eyed Alex sternly. He knew her too well.

Alex folded her arms and sulked. "Yes, I understand," she said grumpily.

Satisfied, Mr. and Mrs. Russo left the restaurant.

"Sorry about that," Alex said, turning to Harper.

"That's okay. I'm sure we can find something superfun yet age-appropriate to do!" Harper replied cheerfully. But her smile faded quickly when she saw the mischievous look on Alex's face.

"Oh, we're still going," Alex told her.

"But your parents said we can't leave the building," Harper reminded Alex.

Alex reached for the book of forbidden spells that she had snuck from Justin's bag. "*Exactly*," she said.

An hour later, Alex and Harper were still in the restaurant—*and* on their way to the party in Brooklyn!

"For the record, I just want to say I think

this is a really, really bad idea!" Harper yelled over the noise of the rumbling subway.

"Only if by *bad*, you mean genius," Alex replied. "I love loopholes."

With the help of the forbidden spell book, Alex had detached the old subway car that was part of her family's restaurant. Now she and Harper were traveling to the party by way of the New York City transit system!

As they sped through the underground tunnels, Harper tried to keep the dishes and silverware from falling off the rocking tables. Then she saw the lights from an oncoming train. It was heading right for them!

"Alex!" Harper shouted.

Thankfully, at the last possible second, the oncoming train magically swerved onto another track.

"Can't you slow it down?" Harper cried.

"Uh . . . no," Alex responded. "When my parents put in the tables, I think they took out the controls. But don't worry, it's *enchanted*. It knows where it's going."

Harper glanced out the window again.

"Then why are we heading *uptown*?" she asked as she watched the stations flash by. "Forty-second Street. Forty-ninth. Fifty-seventh. Brooklyn is in the other direction *and* on the other side of the river."

Alex stamped her foot. "Stupid spell. Oh, wait! My bad. I had the map upside down."

She tapped the subway map with her wand. *"Misguided directions we shouldn't have taken. Hurry up and get us to Bergen Street station!"* she chanted. "These forbidden spells are super–user–friendly," she told Harper.

Suddenly the car came to a screeching halt. The tables—and the girls—went flying! The car moved again, this time in the opposite direction.

"Forbidden spells?" Harper asked Alex. "Why would you use something called a 'forbidden spell'? They're *forbidden*," she said, slightly panicked.

"It's really not a big deal if you have the right wand," Alex told her.

"Do you?" asked Harper.

Alex glanced down at hers. "No. Apparently

it's too powerful. I'm not 'responsible' enough. I can't be 'trusted'—whatever that means." She rolled her eyes. Then she froze as she looked out the front window of the subway car.

"Aaaaaah!" she screamed suddenly. Another train was coming at them on the same track— only this time there was no place for them to swerve! The roar of the train got louder and louder as they got closer. Harper covered her eyes while Alex closed hers—and waved her wand.

The next thing they knew, there was silence. They opened their eyes and saw that they were back at the sub shop.

"I did it!" Alex cried. "I saved us. I can't believe I really did it."

"*You* didn't do it," said Justin, who was standing in front of them with his arms folded. "*I* did."

Harper ran up to Alex's big brother and hugged him. "Oh, Justin, thank you, thank you, thank you!" she cried.

Alex frowned. "Don't thank him. He just

did it so he can run off and tell on me."

"Normally, yes, that *would* be true," Justin said. "But there's no way I'm telling Mom and Dad anything that's going to upset them the night before our vacation. For once, I am not going to let you destroy something important to me."

"Well, then we're good, because they're *definitely* not going to hear about it from me," Alex said.

"And do you know *why* they're not going to hear about it?" Justin continued.

"Didn't we just have this conversation?" Alex asked, confused.

Justin smiled, no longer able to contain his excitement. "I just did my first spell using a full-wizard wand. And, if I must say, I did it *perfectly*."

Justin tapped the wall of the subway car with the silver family wand in satisfaction—then cringed as the whole wall fell apart and crashed to the ground.

Justin shook his head. "*Almost* perfectly," he said with a sigh.

Just then, Mr. and Mrs. Russo walked in and looked around in shock, surveying the scene. Mrs. Russo looked at Alex with disappontment in her eyes.

Alex turned bright red and looked down. I am busted, she thought. *So* busted.

# CHAPTER 2

In a huff, Alex yanked clothes out of a drawer and tossed them in the general direction of the suitcase on her bed.

Standing behind her, Harper sighed. "I'm really sorry you can't stay with me anymore," she told her friend.

"Oh, I was never going to get to stay with you," Alex said. "My mom's been planning this all along. She's just using my innocent borrowing of the diner as an excuse."

"Innocent?" Harper said. "If it wasn't for Justin—"

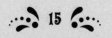

"Harper," Alex interrupted, "your role as my best friend is to blindly agree with me. *And* occasionally say how sorry you are that I have such a mean, *mean* mother."

"Fine." Harper shrugged. "I can do that. You know that's not true, though. You love your mom."

"I didn't say I didn't. I just don't want to spend two weeks in full-on *family* mode." Alex shuddered at the thought. "Someday, I'm going to win the family wizard contest and become a full wizard. Then they're *all* going to be sorry!"

Harper tapped her chin in thought. "What if you fall in love with a mortal and have to give up your powers like your dad did?"

Alex sighed. "I *still* can't believe he did that."

"I can," Harper said. "I love that story. It sounds so romantic."

"It was," Mrs. Russo said, walking into Alex's bedroom.

The girls looked up, startled, to find Mrs. Russo standing by the door. "Do you need any help packing, Alex?" she asked.

"No." Alex turned her back to her mom. "I most definitely do not need *your* help."

"Fine," said Mrs. Russo. "But one of these days I just might not be there to offer it."

Alex turned to look at her mom. She could tell that she'd hurt her feelings. "Mom, I'm sorry," she said. "That isn't what I meant."

"I know what you meant," Mrs. Russo replied. "Finish packing."

Alex grimaced at the mess on her bed—and reached for her wand. In a flash, the clothes jumped inside the suitcase, and the bag closed itself.

"Done!" she exclaimed. Then she saw the frown on her mom's face. She pointed her wand again, and the suitcase went back to the way it was before. "Undone." She grinned. "See what I did there? It's called 'lightening the mood.'"

"Well, I hope you got that out of your system," Mrs. Russo said. "Because I've declared this vacation magic-free." She motioned to Alex's wand. "Hand it over."

Meanwhile, in the next room, Mr. Russo

was delivering the very same news to Alex's brothers.

"I *can't* give up my wand," Max argued. "There are so many spells I haven't done yet!"

"If we give you our wands, we'll only be able to do hand magic," Justin said.

Mr. Russo shook his head. "The idea is *no* magic."

"I can't just *not* do magic for two weeks," Justin protested. "We're going to the Caribbean—one of the most magical places in the entire universe. This is because of Alex, isn't it?" He crossed his arms.

"Well, yeah," Mr. Russo admitted. "And obviously, I'm going to need the family wand back, too."

"No! I'll be good," Justin begged. "I promise. I won't even use it." He pulled the wand out of his pocket. Just then, a sparkling light shot out of it. Suddenly, outside the house, an elephant roared loudly.

Justin winced. "I must have the safety off," he said nervously.

"Why do *we* always suffer when Alex does

something wrong?" Max complained.

"You can't blame Alex for this," Mr. Russo told his sons.

"Oh, yeah? Watch me," Justin said. His face took on an angry expression. "This is me blaming Alex."

But Mr. Russo didn't budge. "It's my fault," he said. "I never should have let you use it in the first place. That wand really is only for full wizards. It's much too powerful and unpredictable. I'm sorry. You understand, right?"

"Yeah, I understand," Justin muttered. Mr. Russo gave the kids a stern look and walked out of the room.

"I *totally* understand," Justin said under his breath. Then he gently patted the silver family wand hidden under his shirt. . . .

"You guys are going to love this resort," Mr. Russo declared the next day. They were piled inside a cab, leaving for the airport.

"It's so beautiful," added Mrs. Russo, turning around in the front seat. "You know that this is where your father and I first met each other."

In the backseat, Alex shot her brothers a look. "She's going to tell it," she groaned.

"Oh, please, don't tell it," Justin begged.

"Did I ever tell you the story . . . ?" their mom began.

Max covered his ears. "She's telling it!"

"It was the summer after I'd graduated from college," Mrs. Russo continued. "I was lying by the pool, and I'd ordered this papaya smoothie—"

"It was a *guava* smoothie," Alex, Justin, and Max muttered in unison.

Their dad nodded in agreement. "Actually, it *was* a guava smoothie."

Mrs. Russo frowned. "Why would I order a guava smoothie?" she asked. "I don't even *like* guava. . . ."

Two hours later, Alex was *still* listening to her mom's story—but this time in an airplane, where escape meant plunging about 25,000 feet straight down. Even worse, she was now trapped between her mom and dad.

"So somehow I spilled papaya all over your father's shirt," Mrs. Russo said.

"Guava," muttered Justin, Alex, and Max.

Three hours later, finally nearing the resort, Alex tried to enjoy the scenery of the island, but it was impossible. Her mom wouldn't stop talking!

"Then I looked up into his eyes, and at that moment I *knew* this was the man for me," Mrs. Russo said with a sigh.

"It was love at first sight," Mr. Russo agreed.

Finally, the cab stopped in front of a luxury hotel.

"We're here!" Alex shouted. "I've never been so happy to get somewhere I didn't want to go in all my life!"

Diving over her father and brother, she tumbled onto the hotel driveway. A uniformed valet helped her to her feet. Beside him, a man held out a tray of tropical drinks.

"Welcome to paradise," he said.

"Sweet!" Max cried, snatching a glass.

"Put that down," his dad ordered. Then he turned to the man serving the drinks. "Are these included in the price?" he asked, money-conscious as always.

The man smiled. "Of course."

Mr. Russo grinned, relieved. "Welcome to the Caribbean, everyone!" he exclaimed, passing the drinks around.

Alex sipped the punch and moved away from her family. The sky was so blue . . . and the beach was so beautiful. . . . Now that she was there, she thought, maybe it wasn't so bad after all. And neither was the cute guy who was handing out the drinks!

"I'm Javier," the guy said, smiling at Alex. "I'm one of the activities counselors."

Alex looked at him and smiled back.

Mrs. Russo hurried over. "That's great, because I already know the first thing we're going to do. Take our picture," she said, motioning to Javier.

Ugh! Alex thought. Family pictures, *already*? Was she going to be able to have *any* fun on this vacation?

# CHAPTER 3

The Russo kids wasted no time unpacking. They were each eager to explore the island further—on their *own*.

"What's going on?" their mother asked, walking into their hotel room. It looked as if all their suitcases had exploded.

"Snorkeling," Max announced, wiggling his rubber flippers. "I like any sport that comes with funny shoes."

Justin waved a copy of *Zapit's Guide to the Caribbean*, a tour book for practicing wizards. "To see the ruins!" he declared. "Did you know

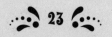

that the most important battles of the first and third Wizard-Troll Wars were fought here?"

"I don't know," Alex said, shrugging. She had no set plan yet. "But I'm getting out while I can."

"No, no, no! This is a *family* vacation," declared Mrs. Russo.

"Your mother's right," said Mr. Russo, walking in behind her. "We should be doing everything together."

"With you? In public? Looking like *that*?" Alex pointed to her dad's bright tropical shirt.

Mr. Russo smirked. "So we're in agreement," he said. "Now, line up for sunblock check!"

Alex groaned. This wasn't a vacation, she decided. It was some ancient form of wizard-in-training torture!

The morning of "family togetherness" began with a snorkeling trip. It ended with Justin's guided tour of an ancient fort's ruins. The whole time, their mom snapped enough photos to fill at least twenty photo albums.

The next day, family together time resumed bright and early.

"Don't you just love the ancient walls and the cobblestone streets?" Mrs. Russo asked Alex as they walked along. "Your father and I walked along here on one of our first dates."

"It must have been pretty when it was new," Alex muttered.

"Listen," Mrs. Russo said, "this attitude—"

"I'm sorry," Alex said defensively, "but memory lane is turning out to be the longest road in the world! When do I get to do something *I* want to do?" she complained.

"You're right," her mom said, thinking it over. "You haven't gotten to pick yet. You can choose next. But you have to at least start *pretending* that you want to be here. Deal?"

Alex thought for a moment. Then she remembered the cute activities director.

Suddenly, Justin rushed up to his sister and held up his guidebook. "Look at this!" he exclaimed excitedly. "'The Top One Hundred Must-See Wizard Sights on the Island.' I wonder why we haven't seen any of them.

Oh, wait, I know." Justin paused and looked straight at Alex. "You," he said. He refused to let her forget that it was her fault they hadn't been allowed to bring their wands or do any magic on the vacation.

"You want magic?" Alex asked. "*There's* magic." She pointed across the way to a magician with a parrot perched on his shoulder. He had set up a small table and a sandwich board that read THE AMAZING ARCHIE. At that moment, it looked as if he was in the middle of a rather *un*-amazing card trick.

"And now my gorgeous assistant, Giselle, will reveal your card," the magician told a tourist "volunteer." The parrot on the magician's shoulder reached for the card with her beak, and Alex and Justin could hear him whisper to her, "Not that one. Not that one, either." Finally, the parrot selected a card and pulled it out of the deck.

"The three of clubs!" Archie announced. "What do you say? Pretty amazing, is what I say!" The few people who were watching applauded politely.

"Pretty pathetic, is what I say," Justin muttered.

Max walked up to his older siblings and put his arm around them. "You know what the trouble with you two is?" he asked. "You don't know how to make your *own* fun." And with that, Max marched off toward the magician.

"I'll volunteer," he told Archie.

"Okay, wasn't really asking for volunteers…" the magician began. "But sure," he said. "Have you got any money?" he asked hopefully.

Max tossed a few coins into the magician's empty hat.

"Okay, first, I'll need your drink," the magician said.

"Why?" Max asked, handing him the can of soda he'd been drinking.

"Because I'm doing eight shows a day in the blazing sun," the magician replied. He took a sip and handed Max a balloon. "Here. Blow this up," he said.

Max blew up the balloon and handed it back to the magician.

"Okay, kids, don't try this at home," the

magician said, pulling a large knitting needle out of his sleeve. He was just about to pierce the balloon when it suddenly began to lift him into the air! Max motioned discreetly for it to keep rising, while the magician held on for dear life.

"Max!" cried Mrs. Russo, as soon as she realized what was going on. Before Max could bring the balloon down, however, the magician reached up and popped it himself with his knitting needle.

"Now *that's* a good trick," the magician said after making a fairly good landing, complete with a tuck and roll. "You and I need to—" he began to say to Max. But just then, a police officer stepped into view. The magician quickly folded up his sign and his table. "I'm going, I'm going," the magician told the cop.

Mr. and Mrs. Russo, meanwhile, glared at their youngest son.

"Hey, is it my fault the guy's a really good magician?" Max asked, trying to act innocent. But his parents knew better. "I'm sorry," he said with a sigh, "But it's not like it's a big deal! It was training magic. No one's going to figure out we're wizards."

Just then, the magician appeared beside them. "You're *wizards*!" he cried.

"Okay, maybe one person," Max said.

Mr. Russo froze. Then he tried to laugh it off. "What? No. That's very funny. We are most definitely *not—*"

"Don't even try it," the magician interrupted. "Do you actually think if I could do that trick on my own I'd be hustling tourists for loose change?"

"Kids, let's go," Mrs. Russo said quickly. She tried to walk them away while the parrot squawked loudly in the magician's ear.

"What? Oh, right!" the magician replied. "I'm leaving out the most important part. We're wizards, too!" he said excitedly. The whole Russo family exchanged looks.

"You're *wizards*?" Justin asked. "I don't think so." After all, the magician barely seemed able to do *mortal* magic. And a wizard *parrot*? Who'd ever heard of that?

"Well, not now, obviously," Archie said.

"But we used to be. I swear! Wizard's honor." He raised his hand, and the parrot raised her wing. "I was born a wizard," he told the group. "But I lost out in the family wizard competition. Done in by a know-it-all older brother."

Max and Alex both looked at Justin. "I know the feeling," they said in unison.

"And my poor, lovely Giselle here was transformed into her current feathery state by an evil—" The magician stopped as the parrot nipped him on the ear. "Right. Not telling that part of the story," he said.

"Well, it was great running into you," said Mr. Russo with a wave. "Good luck with the magic thing. Everybody into the van," he told the kids.

"Wait!" Archie cried. He moved to block their way, "magically" producing a business card from his hand. "I could show you some of the wizarding sights!" he exclaimed. "I'm also an excellent, reasonably priced tour guide. Tips are *greatly* encouraged."

"Really?" asked Justin, suddenly *very* interested.

"Oh, no," Mrs. Russo said. "It's Alex's turn to choose. And I just know it's going to be something *far* away from here."

Alex nodded, thinking of an afternoon windsurfing with Javier.

"But—" Justin watched, dejected, as his family marched off toward the van.

"I could show you *La Piedra de los Sueños*," Archie called after them.

Justin stopped and spun around. *"The Stone of Dreams?"* He gasped.

Archie nodded. "I know where it is. We have a map."

Justin quickly ripped through his guidebook. "That's like the most *important* wizard artifact *ever*!" he exclaimed. "It can do *anything*. Do you really know where it is? Dad!" Justin cried. "They have a map to the Stone of Dreams!"

"Yeah, so does every other wizard gift shop in town," Mr. Russo said, walking back over toward Justin. "And every year one or two idiot wizards go traipsing through the jungle looking for the stone and end up getting themselves killed." He shot Archie an angry look.

"Please," Archie begged him, "we're desperate! We've been on this island for years, just hoping to meet another wizard who could help us. The stone is the only hope of restoring Giselle to her former, beautiful . . ." Archie paused. "Less *feathery* state."

"I'm sorry," Mr. Russo said. "It's just too dangerous. Come on, Justin."

Justin clenched his fists. "But Dad . . ."

"The stone doesn't even exist," Mr. Russo told him. He put his hands on Justin's shoulders and gently guided him away. "And you've got to have done something pretty bad to have yourself turned into a bird," he whispered.

Giselle squawked angrily in the magician's ear as they watched them go.

"I didn't really have a choice, now, did I?" Archie shot back. "Trust me, I know what I'm doing," he went on.

Squawk!

"Yes, there's a first time for everything. Very funny," Archie huffed.

# CHAPTER 4

Alex hopped off her surfboard and hit the water with a splash. She surfaced a few seconds later. Now *this* is a vacation, she thought to herself happily, bobbing on the clear blue waves. She didn't even care that she'd been struggling with her surfboard board for basically the whole afternoon.

Javier didn't seem to mind, either. Although he was supposed to be giving windsurfing lessons to the entire Russo family, his attention was totally focused on Alex.

"Don't worry, you'll get it," he told her,

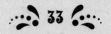

flashing her a smile. "I wasn't very good my first time, either."

"I'm just having a little problem with the *wind* part. And the *surfing* part. And the *standing-up* part," Alex said jokingly.

Javier laughed, just as Justin cruised by on his own board.

"Watch and learn!" Justin called out.

Alex glared in his direction. Show-off! she thought. "Forbidden-shmidden," she mumbled. She'd show him! She focused her powers and began to chant, *"Though a surfboard I might be a mess on, my brother is in need of a less-on!"*

Then she pursed her lips and blew.

Suddenly, a powerful gust of wind ripped across the shoreline. Waves kicked up and surfers started falling off their boards. Justin's surfboard caught the breeze and began to zip across the water. He cringed as his board headed straight for a huge wave. Luckily, Justin had a secret weapon. He reached into his life vest . . . and pulled out the family wand.

Justin pointed the wand at his board,

which instantly began to glow, and the next thing he and Alex knew, he was flying up, over the wave, doing a perfect somersault, and landing gracefully on the other side.

"Wow. Go Justin!" Mrs. Russo called out.

"He's a natural," Javier commented.

"Yeah, a natural *idiot*," Alex grumbled to herself. "He's got the wand." Cheater!

Later that day, Javier caught up with Alex near the resort's outdoor restaurant. She smiled and thanked him again for the windsurfing lesson.

"There's a party down the beach later," he told her. "Any chance I could talk you into going with me?"

Alex nodded. "A *huge* chance." Then she sighed. "Unfortunately, my mother isn't so easily persuaded. But I'll work something out."

She flashed him a smile as he walked away. She turned to find her mother standing behind her.

"What are you 'working out'?" Mrs. Russo asked curiously.

Alex smiled slyly. "How sweet I have to be for you to let me go to a party," she replied.

"With *him*?" Mrs. Russo asked. "It's *so* not happening."

Alex threw up her hands. "Why can't I go?" she complained.

"*First* of all, we—all of us together—are on vacation," her mom told her.

Alex pouted. "More like a never-ending photo shoot," she complained.

"I'm trying to make *memories*," her mom explained. "And second, I said *no*. You don't need to be spending any more time with that boy—"

"But you hardly even know him!" Alex cried.

Mrs. Russo placed her hands on her hips. "I know he's too old for you. That he probably hits on every girl who comes to this resort. And, at best, he's just trying to hustle you into taking more windsurfing lessons." And with that, she turned to go.

Alex stood there, fists clenched, with her face getting redder and redder. Her mother was *so* impossible. It was like she didn't want Alex to have any life at all! Why couldn't she even see her side of things? Hmm, thought Alex, maybe with a little magic, she could.

She took a deep breath and began to chant softly under her breath.

*"A party I must attend, on that we can't agree. But for a refreshing change, today you'll side with me!"*

Mrs. Russo suddenly turned around and walked back to her daughter. "You know what?" she said to Alex. "You're young. Go. Have a good time." Alex grinned, and then Mrs. Russo suddenly shook her head. "What am I saying? Absolutely not! Now, come on, everybody's waiting."

Alex sighed. "Darn," she muttered. "Not enough juice."

Reluctantly, Alex followed her mom to the buffet. Her dad and brothers were already there, filling their plates. As they sat down and ate, the kids were treated to *more* stories—this time from *Mr.* Russo.

"And we were sitting right here when I

told your mother that I was a wizard," he was saying.

Mrs. Russo smiled. "He also told me he loved me."

Max shook his head. "Why would you do that?" he asked his dad. "Didn't you know you were going to have to give up your magic?"

"It wasn't that important," Mr. Russo replied.

Spare me, Alex thought. But she tried to play along. "That was beautiful," she said flatly. "I'm tearing up." She made a show of wiping her eyes, then grabbed her plate. "Okay, who wants some more pork? Justin? Good. Come with." Then she grabbed him by the arm and yanked him away.

Justin followed Alex to the buffet. But before he could refill his plate, his sister confronted him.

"I know you have the wand," she said accusingly.

"What? No, I . . ." Justin stuttered. Then his eyes narrowed suspiciously. "You went through my stuff again," he said accusingly.

"Didn't have to," said Alex. "There's no way you could have stayed on that wind-surfer." She puckered her lips and blew, and Justin glowered.

"*You?*" he said. "But it's almost impossible to do weather spells without a wand . . . unless . . . *you* have the spell book!" he cried.

Alex smiled mischievously.

"You're not even going to try and deny it?" Justin asked.

"Why?" said Alex. It was part of her new plan, after all. "Here's the fun blackmail part," she told him. "Let *me* use the wand, or I tell Dad you really did take it without permission this time."

Justin shrugged. "I'll just tell him *you* took the spell book," he replied.

"So?" said Alex. "I'm not the good one."

Justin squirmed. She was right.

"Please," Alex added. "I found this amazing 'agreement spell' that'll make Mom and Dad agree to anything for six hours. But I don't have enough power on my own. I need the wand."

"Just tell *me* the spell," Justin suggested. "I already have enough power."

"No way!" Alex exclaimed. Where was the fun in that? Besides, agreeing with goody-two-shoes Justin was basically the same as agreeing with Mom and Dad. "Justin, come on," she begged. "I can go to my party, and you can go on whatever magical mystery tour you want. Win-win. They'll never know."

But her brother shook his head. "Then let *me* do it," he told her.

Alex sighed. "Fine. *You* sneak out of dinner, do a forbidden spell, and risk eternal grounding."

Justin frowned. "Right," he said. "*You* go." He wasn't the good one for nothing. "I'll keep everyone occupied."

So Justin returned to the table and Alex dashed back to her room with the wand. She opened the spell book and began to recite the magic words: "*A party I must attend. On that we can't agree. But for a refreshing change—*"

"Alex?" said Mrs. Russo, coming up behind her.

"Mom!" Alex cried, spinning around. "What are you doing here?"

"The minute Justin tried to magically glue me to my chair, I knew something was up," her mom replied. She eyed the silver wand and the open book on the bed. "You just will not stop, will you?" she said, shaking her head.

Alex could see that her mother was angry, but she was pretty mad, too. "Well, what am I supposed to do—since you've decided you're going to control every single second of my life!"

"Oh, please," her mom said with a sigh. "Do you think I'm doing this for *me*?"

"I'm sixteen." Alex stomped her foot. "You can't keep telling me what to do."

Mrs. Russo crossed her arms. "Watch me," she said. "For the rest of this trip, you are going to be pleasant and . . ."

"You can't make me," Alex challenged.

"And when we get home, you are grounded for two months," Mrs. Russo added. "No dating. No parties. No *magic*."

"*Mom!*" Alex wailed.

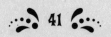 41

"Not another word," her mom said. "I've had it." She nodded to the book and the wand in Alex's hand. "Now put those things away. We're all going to this little place where I taught your dad how to salsa." Then she turned her back on her daughter and walked into the next room.

Alex was really mad now. Frustration and rage were coursing through her body like a river of molten lava. "Ahh!" she yelled, tapping into a power she didn't even know she had. "I hate you! I wish you and Dad had never even met!"

Then, all of a sudden, light started shooting from the wand in her hand. Alex had forgotten she was still holding it. She looked down at the spell book, which was glowing, too—and around at the room, which was rippling with magical energy.

When Alex spoke again, her voice was barely audible. "What did you just do?" she asked the wand. "That wasn't a *spell*." Then she dropped it on the bed and ran out of the room. This was *so* not good.

# CHAPTER 5

Alex hurried into the adjoining room and breathed a sigh of relief when she saw her mom talking on the phone. Everything seemed to be perfectly normal.

"Is everything okay?" Alex asked when Mrs. Russo hung up.

Her mother spun around. "Oh, you startled me," she said. "I didn't think you'd get here so quickly."

Alex frowned. "But I was just next door."

Her mother pointed to her dad's suitcases, which were tucked into a corner. "Well, like I told the guy at the front desk, they accidentally brought some guy's luggage to my room. Get rid of it, will you?" she said.

"What?" Alex blinked in confusion.

"Aren't you a little young to be a concierge?" her mother asked her. Then she shrugged. "But it probably means you know all the great party spots. Am I right?" She grinned. "I'll definitely be talking to you later. And if you see the maid," she added, grabbing her purse, "tell her I need more towels."

Speechless, Alex watched her mom walk out of the room, and her whole body froze in panic. This couldn't *really* be happening, could it? she thought. Did her mother *really* not know her? At *all*?

Alex knew that she had to find Justin—and fast!

"Justin," she called, waving him down outside the resort's restaurant.

"Alex, what's wrong?" Justin asked.

"Nothing. Why?" she said quickly. "Does

something seem wrong? Where's Dad?" she demanded.

"I don't know," Justin said, throwing his hands up. "Mom left. And then he left. And nobody came back. Did you do the spell?" he asked.

Alex bit her lip. "Uh, I did *a* spell."

"That's great. Did it work?" Justin asked. But before Alex could answer, he spotted their dad approaching. "Hey," Justin called to his father. "I'm going to skip all the family stuff for the rest of the trip and just concentrate on the ruins, okay?"

Mr. Russo looked at him and shrugged. "Sounds good, dude. I say, do what you got to do." Then he gave Justin a fist bump and strolled on.

Justin gasped. "Did Dad just call me *dude*?" he asked.

Just then, their mom rounded a corner, nearly bumping into their dad. The two did a little side step, then walked on without speaking.

"And how come Mom and Dad don't seem

to know each other?" Justin asked Alex, his eyes narrowing.

Before she could reply, however, they both watched their dad walk by a potted plant. He pointed at it and it suddenly bloomed!

"And *why* does Dad have *magic*?" Justin demanded. "Dad is not supposed to have magic! Alex, what have you *done*?"

"*See*?" Alex shot back. "This is what you get for letting *me* use the wand."

But this was no time to argue. They had to reverse the spell. And to do that they needed the family wand and *The Book of Forbidden Spells*. But when they returned to their hotel room, both were gone!

"Are you sure this is where you left them?" Justin asked as he pulled the beds apart.

"Yeah . . ." said Alex, just as Max walked in.

"Thanks for ditching me," he said to Justin and Alex. "Once I ate everyone's dessert, I kind of started to get worried."

Justin folded his arms. "Alex, do you want to tell our little brother what you did?"

he asked. Then he blurted out, "She got into a huge fight with Mom and used the family wand—"

"That *you* gave me," Alex interrupted.

"That is not my fault!" Justin shot back.

"She wished that Mom and Dad had never met and now they haven't. It's like it was twenty years ago. They don't know *us*. They don't know each *other*," he told Max.

Max scratched his head. "So we don't have parents? I'm confused. Is this a good thing or a bad thing?"

Alex raised an eyebrow. "Kid's got a point."

"It's a very *bad* thing!" Justin exclaimed. "And this is why I don't do bad things, because whenever I do, more bad things happen."

"So," Alex replied, "you're admitting it's kind of your fault."

Justin ignored his sister's last comment. He circled the room one last time, searching for the wand and book. "They're not here," he concluded. "So there's only one place they could be."

* * *

Later on, the kids found their father sitting near the pool. And sure enough, *The Book of Forbidden Spells* was sticking out of his back pocket!

"See," Justin told Alex and Max. "Since he hasn't met Mom, Dad never had to give up his powers. He's still a wizard."

Alex nodded. "If we can look at that book, I'm sure we can figure out how to reverse the spell." She paused. "If we all want it reversed?"

Justin gave her a stern look. "Yes," he said.

"Just checking," Alex replied.

Just then, Max spotted his mom walking toward the pool. "You're both making this *way* too complicated," he told his brother and sister. "She's *Mom*. She'll know who I am!"

Before they could stop him, Max walked right up to Mrs. Russo. "Hello," he said. "Don't you recognize me?"

"Should I?" Mrs. Russo asked, looking at Max curiously.

"Uh, yeah, it's me!" he cried. "Max. Maximum. Maxie. The cutest little guy in the whole world? Or was that just a bunch of words to you?" he asked, frowning.

Mrs. Russo started to back away. "If I knew there'd be so many kids around, I'd never have booked this place," she commented.

Max was crushed. "You *really* don't know who I am?"

"No idea. Sorry," his mom replied with a shrug. She turned to walk away, but then Max ran up to her and gave her a giant hug. Mrs. Russo didn't know what to do.

Justin and Alex hurried over to pull Max away. Justin then turned his attention to his dad.

From behind a potted fern, the three siblings watched him sitting near the pool and eyed his back pocket.

"We just need a simple levitation spell," Justin whispered.

Max cracked his knuckles. "Please. That's my specialty."

Justin frowned. "You have no specialty."

But he let his little brother give it a try.

With a flick of his hand, Max magically lifted the book out of Mr. Russo's pocket. All seemed fine—until Mr. Russo spun around, and the kids found themselves yanked out from their hiding places, as if by an invisible force, and lined up in front of him.

"*Nobody* touches the book," he told them. Then he chuckled, looking down at their nervous faces.

"I totally had you! So what have I got? A couple of young wizards pulling a prank?" Mr. Russo asked eagerly.

"Something like that," Justin replied.

Mr. Russo nodded approvingly. "Excellent. I once turned my math teacher into a golden retriever. Never got caught," he said with a mischievous smile.

Just then, a waitress walked up to the group, setting down a plate in front of Mr. Russo.

"One order of *grande* nachos," she said with a smile.

"Thanks a *mucho*," Mr. Russo said, smiling

back. When the bartender was gone, he waved his hand and the plate of nachos quadrupled in size.

"The portions here are so small," he told the kids with a shrug.

Max's jaw dropped. "You just did magic for *fun*?" he asked incredulously. Wasn't that just what their dad always told them *not* to do?

Mr. Russo grinned. "Hey, you guys want anything to eat?" he asked. "On me. It's just money, right?"

Now it was Alex who was speechless. "Where was that attitude when I wanted my own phone?" she asked.

"Tell me about it," her dad replied. "Parents can be such jerks!"

"Hey, for no particular reason, just making conversation—I don't suppose you've got a silver wand on you?" Alex asked him.

"I *so* do!" Mr. Russo exclaimed. The wand instantly appeared in his hand. "I just won my family wizard contest. I've got more power than you could ever imagine."

He held out his hands, and his palms glowed for a second. "How cool is *that*?" he boasted. "People always say magic isn't everything. Well, you know what? They're lying. Magic for everybody!" he shouted. He casually pointed the wand toward a pair of steel drums. Suddenly, music started to blare out of the instruments.

Justin looked over at his dad and gave him a serious look. "Being that you're a full wizard, maybe you could answer a question," Justin said.

Mr. Russo shrugged.

"Suppose a young, inexperienced, *selfish* wizard—" Justin started to say.

"He gets it," Alex interrupted.

"*Accidentally* wished that two people had never met. How would you undo that?" Justin asked him.

His dad chewed thoughtfully. "Beats me," he said. "Good thing that wasn't on the exam. But I know they'd have to do something fast to prevent serious, permanent damage," he said.

"Serious?" Max asked, concerned.

"Permanent?" asked Alex.

"Damage?" Justin said.

"You know, like if the two people had kids," their dad explained. "Eventually reality would catch up, and the kids would disappear forever. No meet. No kids. Simple logic."

Max's eyes widened.

"How soon?" Alex asked.

Mr. Russo shrugged again. "I don't know. Forty-eight hours? But they'd know before it was going to happen because they'd start to forget everything about their past."

The Russo kids stood quietly, all of them in shock, running through their life histories in their minds.

"They'd need a miracle," Mr. Russo continued.

"A miracle," Justin murmured, "*or* the Stone of Dreams."

"The Stone of Dreams?" Mr. Russo asked. "Oh, yeah, that would do it. Supposedly it can grant any wish and reverse any spell, but you only get *one* chance. That would be a fun adventure, looking for that thing."

"Isn't it dangerous?" Justin asked, remembering what the father he had *once* known had said.

"So?" his dad replied. "Is he always like this?" Mr. Russo asked Alex, pointing to Justin. And with that, he took off for the beach, leaving his three kids behind to wonder what to do next.

# CHAPTER 6

It was nighttime, but since their mom and dad now had *both* of their hotel rooms, the Russo kids had no choice but to spend the night on the beach. Alex lucked out and got a hammock, but she didn't feel so lucky when Justin and Max flipped her out of it the next morning.

"Alex!" Justin shouted.

"I'm up," she groaned, brushing sand off herself as she stumbled to her feet. "So, what's your plan?"

"Oh, I get it," Justin said, annoyed. "You

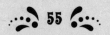

thought I'd come up with something? That you'd wake up, and miraculously problem solved?"

Alex shrugged. "I was kind of hoping . . ." she said, her voice trailing off. She and Max both looked at Justin, who sighed and crossed his arms.

"*Of course* I thought of something!" Justin exclaimed.

Max and Alex grinned. "Okay," Justin continued. "So here's the plan. Alex and I find the Stone of Dreams, while Max stays here and makes sure Mom and Dad don't get into any trouble."

"They're old," Max said, wrinkling his nose. "What kind of trouble could they get into?"

"Uh, I don't know," Justin said sarcastically. "They could meet other people, fall in love, get married . . ."

Max covered his ears. "Okay, I got it! I won't let them out of my sight."

A few hours later, Alex and Justin were sitting at a table in the resort's outdoor café.

Sitting across from them was Archie, the magician they had met earlier, and his parrot, Giselle.

Archie was about to show them the map he had tried to show them before. With a flourish, he pulled out a rolled-up piece of parchment and unfurled it.

"Here you go," Archie said, handing the map to Justin.

"The map to the Stone of Dreams. I can't believe it," Justin murmured.

"I knew you'd call," Archie told him. "That you wouldn't let us down. When I told you about the map, Giselle's feathers were all in a ruffle. She never thinks I know what I'm doing."

Alex peered over Justin's shoulder. "This is a flyer for the all-you-can eat special at the Crab Shack," she told Archie.

"Oops," Archie said. "Don't want to lose that. They have the best flan on the island." He quickly took the flyer back from Justin and handed him a second roll of parchment.

Justin glanced at the map and then looked

up at Archie. "You're sure this map is real?" he asked.

Archie nodded. "Absolutely. It's the only one in the world."

Just then, the kids noticed their dad walking toward their table. "Hey, guys! Look what I just bought!" he exclaimed. He reached into a bag and pulled out a map that looked almost identical to Archie's. "Isn't it cool?" Mr. Russo asked. "You totally inspired me to find the stone. I'll let you know how it goes." He smiled and walked away.

"Where's Max?" Justin asked, frowning.

Suddenly Max appeared, panting, beside them. "Jerry, wait up!" he called. "They're just like roaches," he told Justin and Alex. "You corner one of them, and the other takes off in the opposite direction."

Max hurried after Mr. Russo, and Justin and Alex turned back to Archie.

"The only one in the world, huh?" Alex asked, folding her arms and glaring at Archie.

Archie smiled but didn't reply. He reached

behind Alex's ear and pulled out a small scrap of parchment.

"Those other maps don't work," he said, "because nobody else knows where to start." He put the scrap of paper on the corner of his map. The pieces lined up perfectly to reveal a picture of a gargoyle that marked the trail's secret starting point.

Justin and Alex leaned in closer. We need to be there, the young wizards thought. And in the blink of an eye, Alex, Justin, Archie, and Giselle were at the place pictured on the map!

Suddenly, the group was standing in the middle of a jungle.

An old stone marker in the shape of a gargoyle stood in front of Alex—just like the marker pictured on the map. But as far as she could tell, there was no path to follow at all.

"All right, let's move, people," Justin ordered. "We don't have a lot of time!" He looked around the thickets of trees and shrubs. "Which way?" He gulped nervously.

Alex studied the map, frowning. "There's writing," she said. "But it doesn't make any sense."

"That's because the writing's in Spanish," Justin explained, "which you've only been taking since the *second* grade."

Alex sighed. "I kind of peaked at *habla español*," she said with a sigh.

Justin read the words and began to translate. "It says that the path will only reveal itself to the one whose intentions are pure." He smirked. "So, *me*, obviously," he quipped.

"Normally, I'd object," Alex said. "But even I can't make that argument."

Justin picked up the gargoyle-shaped stone and focused intently on it.

"Show me the way," he commanded. "Open up. Reveal the path!"

They held their breath, waiting for the path to open.

"Maybe I'm translating it wrong. Here, hold this," Justin said, handing the marker off to Alex. "I'll get my Spanish dictionary." But just as he reached into his backpack,

Alex Russo really wanted to go to a party with her best friend, Harper Evans, even though Alex's mom said no.

Mrs. Russo dragged Alex to the Caribbean for their family vacation. Alex was *not* happy about it.

The Russos met a magician named Archie.
He told them about the Stone of Dreams.

Alex wanted to cast a spell on her mom so that she could do whatever she wanted during their vacation.

"When we get home, you are grounded for two months," Mrs. Russo told Alex when she caught her using magic.

Alex's wish had come true. Neither of her parents remembered their kids—or each other.

"The Stone of Dreams can grant any wish and reverse any spell," Mr. Russo told them.

Justin studied the map Archie gave him that would help them find the magical stone.

"What if we don't get to the stone in time and can't save everyone?" Alex asked Justin worriedly.

Mr. and Mrs. Russo headed into the jungle
to look for Alex and Justin.

Finally, Alex and Justin found the stone. But just then, Archie's
parrot, Giselle, swooped in and grabbed it!

In order to try and reverse the spell, Alex and Justin would have to compete against each other to see who was a better wizard.

"Wands at the ready," Mr. Russo announced.
"Ready. Set. Magic!"

After an intense battle, Alex won the competition.

"I want everything to be exactly the way it was," Alex said.
Her family was saved!

the stone started to glow! Alex looked down at the stone in her hands in shock, and then looked even *more* surprised as a path suddenly opened up.

"I did it," Alex said slowly, her eyes wide with amazement.

Justin scowled. "*You* didn't do anything. It must have been a delayed reaction." He shoved his dictionary back into his backpack. "Come on."

Meanwhile, back at the resort, Max Russo was on a solo mission.

I've got to find a way to get my mom and dad to fall in love again, he thought. Then we won't even *need* that old magic stone! First mission objective: track down Mom!

Max found Mrs. Russo lounging by the pool. He still couldn't believe that one little spell could wipe away her entire memory.

"What kind of mother doesn't even remember her own kid?" Max muttered to himself. "The other two, sure, I get that. But *me* . . . I'm her favorite!"

Just then, Max noticed a man walking up to talk to his mom.

"Who's that?" Max asked a pool attendant.

"That's my boss, the activities director," the guy replied. "He's just signing her up for windsurfing lessons."

"Oh," Max said with a sigh of relief.

"Or *flirting*," the guy added. "He's kind of shameless."

*Uh-oh*, Max thought. He had to handle this! But how?

Glancing around the pool area, he noticed a large cart loaded with towels. He smiled. *Got it*, he thought.

Moments later, Max crashed the cart into the man, flipping him into the big towel bin and sending him rolling away.

Max approached his mom. "What do you think you're doing?" he asked.

"*You* again," she said.

"Do you even know that guy?" Max asked.

Mrs. Russo sighed. "This place has got to get some security."

Just then, Max spotted his dad taking a seat nearby.

"Look," Max told his mom, "if you want to talk to somebody, talk to *that* guy."

Mrs. Russo glanced in the direction Max was pointing in. "He looks like he's doing fine on his own," she said.

Huh? Max turned to see his dad talking to a pretty waitress.

"Oh, for . . ." Max grumbled. "I'll be right back," he told his mom. "Stay here. Mind your own business. Order a smoothie—and wait for love at first sight."

Mrs. Russo rolled her eyes. "I could be here a long time."

"Not as long as you think," Max promised.

# CHAPTER 7

**B**ack in the jungle, Justin continued to lead the group, but their progress was getting slower.

Alex pushed her way through a tangle of branches. "How'd she get turned into a parrot, anyway?" Alex asked Archie, eyeing Giselle.

"It's quite a story, actua—" Archie began. But he was quickly interrupted when Giselle bit his finger—hard! *"Ouch!* That would be my finger!" he cried. "I don't know, really," he muttered to Alex.

Up ahead, Justin was studying his

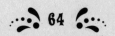

compass. "We should be going six degrees north by northeast," he mumbled, trying to correctly translate Spanish into English. "We follow this for ten paces . . . and *stop*. Now we need to go—"

"Justin," Alex complained, walking up behind him. "Kind of in a *hurry*." She tapped her watch. "Time rippling. Us disappearing!" she reminded him.

Justin stopped and turned around. "I swear, you can't go two seconds without criticizing me!" he exclaimed. "Would you please just let me do this my way?"

Alex sighed. "Why do you have to do everything the way you do magic?"

"You mean perfectly?" Justin asked.

"I mean *annoyingly*," Alex replied.

"There's a *right* way to do things, and that's the way I like to do them," Justin told her. "You might want to try it sometime." He paused before proceeding. Then he looked at Alex oddly.

"Why are you getting taller?" he asked her.

"Because," Alex said, "you couldn't stop

being perfect long enough to notice that you're standing in *quicksand*."

Justin glanced down. He was up to his knees in mud and sinking fast! "Alex! Help me! Get me out of here!" he cried.

Instead of helping him, however, Alex grabbed the map out of his hand. "Okay, maybe *now* we can get someplace," she said.

"Alex!" Justin shouted. He tried to grab a low tree branch, but he couldn't reach it.

"So we're here," Alex said as she studied the map, "and we want to go *here*."

"You have it upside down," Justin called out, still trapped in the quicksand.

Alex turned the map around and nodded. "Yeah, that makes more sense." Then she shook her head. "Not really. They need one of those little *X* thingies, like at the mall. Oh, wait, here we are—*bottomless pit of death*." She pointed to the skull and crossbones on the parchment. "And we need to go toward some squiggly things."

"Mountains!" Justin choked, now buried to his shoulders.

"Okay," Alex said. She looked around and saw some hills in the distance. "And there they are! Easy."

"Alex, *please*!" Justin pleaded.

Alex sighed. "Fine," she said. She picked up a branch and held it out, but just as her brother was about to grab it, she lifted it up.

"Can I be in charge of the map?" she asked.

"No," Justin said—as he felt the mud rising to his chin. "Ahhhhh! Okay, *yes*! You can be in charge of the map!"

Alex lowered the branch . . . then once more pulled it out of reach. "Promise?" she asked.

"Yes, yes, I promise!" Justin cried.

Alex grinned and lowered the branch again, and Justin grabbed it and clambered out.

"All right, let's move," Alex said as Justin caught his breath and Archie and Giselle walked up to them. "This way."

Justin rolled his eyes. "The *other* way," he grumbled.

"Fine." Alex spun around. "The *other* this way." She smiled and hiked on.

* * *

Back at the resort, things weren't going much better for Max. He had to get his mom and dad back together. But neither of them seemed interested in falling in love—at least not with each other.

Max walked up to his dad. Mr. Russo, however, was still talking to the waitress at the outdoor restaurant.

Doing his best to act cool, Max sat on a stool next to his father. He noticed that his dad was drinking a smoothie. That gave him his next idea.

"One guava smoothie, please," Max told the waitress.

"We don't make guava smoothies," she replied.

Mr. Russo scratched his head. "Then what am I drinking?" he asked her.

"Papaya," she said.

"All these years," Max complained under his breath. "Get your fruits straight, man!"

When the waitress brought Max's smoothie over to him, he slid the glass toward his father.

"Why don't you take this over to that girl for me—she was asking about you earlier."

Mr. Russo glanced toward the pool and looked over at Mrs. Russo. "Who is that?" he asked. "Your mom?"

"No," Max replied. Then he looked at him hopefully. "Unless you *think* she is and memories are flooding back."

Mr. Russo gave Max a strange look. "You're kind of a weird little kid," he commented.

"Yeah," Max said with a sigh, "I get that a lot. So . . ." He nodded back toward his mom.

But Mr. Russo shook his head. "*Nah*," he said, smiling toward the waitress. "I think I'm good."

Max tried to remain calm. "I'm just saying—you could do *a lot* better." He tilted his head toward the waitress. "She's kind of a dog," he whispered.

"Hey! That's not nice," Mr. Russo scolded. "She's totally—"

Suddenly, Mr. Russo heard a loud bark.

He turned to find the waitress had turned into a golden retriever!

"That's not funny," Mr. Russo told Max. Then he started to snicker. "Okay, it's superfunny. And you totally stole that from me. But you've got to change her back."

Max folded his arms. "As long as you take this smoothie."

Mr. Russo sighed. "Fine," he said, picking up his smoothie and turning to walk away. "But why do you care so—"

Just then there was a giant crash!

Mr. Russo jumped back in surprise. He had knocked right into Mrs. Russo and dumped his smoothie all over her!

For a moment, the two froze. Their eyes locked. *This is it*, Max thought. This was just how his mom and dad had met the first time. Had he totally re-created the moment?

Unfortunately, though, this was not the case.

Mrs. Russo tore her gaze away from Mr. Russo and frowned down at the juice he had spilled all over her. "What is the matter with you?" she snapped.

"I'm sorry," Mr. Russo said. "I didn't see you. I mean, I was just coming over there . . ."

"Why?" she asked. "To throw your drink on me? What did I ever do to you?"

Max squeezed his eyes shut. "Wait," he said, suddenly remembering something. "It's supposed to be the other way around!" Quickly, he pointed toward his mother.

Magic sparks flew through the air. Mrs. Russo grabbed a smoothie off the table and threw it on her husband.

"Hey!" Mr. Russo cried.

Mrs. Russo's eyes widened in surprise. "I'm so sorry," she said. "I don't know why I did that."

Mr. Russo looked at her in confusion. "How could you not know—" he began. Then he noticed Max and guessed what had happened. "You know what?" Mr. Russo told her, "Don't worry about it. We're even."

Mrs. Russo began to say something, but she changed her mind. She turned and walked the other way.

"Go after her!" Max urged him. "You like her, right?"

Mr. Russo gazed in the direction Mrs. Russo had walked in. "Cute and feisty?" He nodded and grinned. "She's *totally* my type. I could so fall for her—*if* she were a wizard."

"What?!" Max gasped. That was the last thing he expected his dad to say! "What does that matter?"

"I told you," Mr. Russo said, "I just became a full wizard. I'm not going to give it up for some *mortal*."

"But—" Max began.

"Very sticky," Mr. Russo said, pointing to his wet shirt. "I've got to go."

Max watched him, then turned back to the waitress, who was still transformed into a golden retriever. She barked loudly.

Oh, man, Max thought. *That* plan totally backfired. What am I going to do now?

# CHAPTER 8

Deep in the jungle, Alex and Justin were leading the way. Archie and Giselle followed behind them. While Justin and Alex argued over directions yet again, Archie took the opportunity to talk to Giselle privately. He could tell that she was angry.

"Giselle," he whispered, "I'm sure if we just asked them not to say anything—"

Giselle interrupted him with a bitter squawk and bit his finger.

"Yes, yes," Archie told her. "I know the wizard authorities sentenced you to fifty years

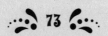

in feathers. But maybe they wouldn't find us if we moved to some remote jungle."

Giselle squawked again.

"But if we take the stone first," Archie reminded the parrot, "they'll disappear forever."

Giselle bobbed her head up and down. And slowly Archie understood. "Which is why it's the *perfect* plan. Wow, you're very good at this," he told the parrot with a sly grin.

Meanwhile, a short distance away, Alex swatted at a bug on her elbow. That was the fifth one in the last five minutes. She was covered in bug bites!

"Are you okay?" Justin asked her.

Alex sighed. "If Mom was still Mom, this never would have happened. She would have told me to put on bug spray."

"So?" Justin shrugged. "You wouldn't have listened."

"True, but at least she'd be telling me, 'I told you so.'" Alex sighed again. "I miss her condescending tone and superior attitude."

Justin laughed. "Remind you of anyone?"

"Yeah. *Mom*," Alex snapped. "Aren't you listening?"

Justin shook his head. "Everything's going to be okay. I promise," he told her.

They turned back to the path and took a few more steps forward, then found themselves emerging from the trees. But suddenly, the path they were on ended. There was nothing but a bottomless canyon, with no bridge as far as they could see!

"What?" cried Justin. He quickly studied the map. "We have to get across *this*? There's no way. It's impossible. It's over. We're totally, completely, hopelessly doom—" He glanced at the map again. "Wait! There are instructions!" Justin waved the parchment under Alex's nose. "It says we have to build a path of stone."

Manual labor? Alex thought. "Never going to happen," she quipped.

"With *magic*," Justin added.

Alex raised her eyebrows. "Okay, *that* might happen."

Sure, construction spells were really

complicated. Especially without a wand or a spell book. But Justin was determined to make this happen.

A dozen attempts later, his spell had finally worked. He gazed admiringly at his very own narrow floating stone bridge.

"I may not be a full wizard," he told his sister. "I might not have the family wand. And *you* were no help whatsoever. But I think this is pretty impressive. All it takes is a superior understanding of hand magic and two semesters of advanced-placement geometry."

Justin glanced at Alex, waiting for her reaction. But she just kept staring blankly at the magic bridge.

"What?" Justin prodded. "No eye-rolling? No coughed 'loser'? No 'get a life'?" Justin smirked. "I'm sorry. I can't hear you. What's that? 'Oh, thank you, Justin. You saved us. You're my hero.'"

Alex looked over at Justin and sighed deeply. She picked up a small pebble and tossed it onto the bridge. *Tink!* Beneath the little pebble, the heavy stones gave way and, one by one, tumbled into the chasm.

Alex cleared her throat. "And may I be the first to say"—she coughed—"*loser*."

Ten minutes later, Alex was suspended above the bottomless gorge. Justin was standing beside her on a single large stone.

"Admit it," she told Justin. "It's not a bad idea." She grinned, but kept her mind focused on keeping the stone beneath them in the air. "It's just a simple levitation spell," Alex said proudly.

Justin didn't respond. He was too intent on keeping another large stone aloft and moving it in front of them. As soon as it was in place, he and Alex leaped from the one stone to the other. They slowly made their way across the canyon.

Justin hated to admit it, but Alex had come through again. He sighed loudly.

Alex shot Justin a curious look. "Why do you always get so mad whenever I get something right?" she asked him.

"Because . . ." Justin shook his head. "It's like you don't even try. You don't even think about it."

She shrugged. "Not thinking works for me."

"Exactly," Justin said. "And it's not fair! I know everything there is to know about magic, but you just do it. This is why I have to study all the time. Usually I'm all 'family wizard,' how could it not be me? Then you come along and do something like this."

"You're not going to lose. Trust me," Alex said. "You'll be the family wizard."

"Don't you even want it?" Justin asked.

Alex thought about it for a second. "I don't know. I don't think I do."

"Really?" he asked. "I know why I want it. I'd be nothing if I wasn't a wizard. Magic is the one thing I'm really, really good at."

"Please," Alex said with a sigh. "You're good at everything. 'Justin's perfect,'" she mimicked. "'Why can't you be more like Justin?'"

"Who says that?" asked Justin.

"Besides you?" Alex asked. "Everyone. Mom and Dad."

"Well, they wouldn't if I wasn't so perfect," he told her.

"You know that's not true. They love you regardless," Alex said.

Justin gave her a doubtful look. Then he smiled at her. "That goes both ways."

Then both of them looked with relief at the solid ground below them. They glanced at the map and prepared to hike on, when a voice called to them from across the canyon.

"Hello!" It was Archie, still standing on the other side. "Don't forget about your trusty and loyal guides!" he called. "If you could just slide those rocks—"

But it was too late. They all watched as the floating rocks suddenly fell away. *Oops!* thought Justin and Alex.

"There's not enough time," Justin called back to Archie. "We'll come back for you after we get the stone!"

Archie watched them disappear into the far jungle, then looked up to see Giselle swoop down, holding a long vine in her beak.

"Climb down *there*?" Archie gulped,

peeking over the side of the canyon. "Well, yes, that does seem to be our only—"

*Squaaaaaaaaawk!*

"Have I ever mentioned to you my fear of heights? Not caring . . . All right, then . . ." Archie said slowly. And then he began to make his way down the side of the cliff.

# CHAPTER 9

After the smoothie incident, Max lost track of his parents for a few hours. When he finally saw his mom again, she was wearing a pretty sundress and sandals.

Max followed her down to the resort's dock area. On the way, he caught sight of his dad. "Where have you been?" Max demanded, running up to him.

Mr. Russo held up a racket. "Tennis lesson."

Max folded his arms. "Well, it sounds like *you've* just got money to burn," he said,

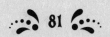

repeating something his dad had said to him many times before.

Mr. Russo leaned closer to the young wizard. "If you go to the restaurant tonight, don't have the cold noodles." He paused to laugh. "At nine o'clock they're going to turn into worms."

"*Really*? Pasta into worms." Max rolled his eyes at such a childish prank—something else his dad would never have done before. "The dad I know would never let me get away with something like that."

"I know," Mr. Russo said with a shrug. "Mine either." Just then, he noticed Max's "Big Apple" T-shirt. "Hey, you from New York? Me, too."

Max looked down at his T-shirt. "Yeah, I guess." He scratched his head. "Actually, I can't remember where I was born." Max blinked. *Uh-oh*, he thought. The first stage of disappearing—I'm starting to forget my past!

Looking up, Max realized that his dad was walking away. And his mom was now heading in the other direction.

He ran up to his mother. "Wait!" he cried. "Where are you going?"

"None of your business," she replied coolly. "Look, I know what this is about."

"You do?" Max asked hopefully.

Mrs. Russo pointed to her husband, who was heading toward the pool. "You want to set me up with your friend—but trust me, he couldn't be less interested."

"That's not true!" Max declared. "He told me that you're *totally* his type. I'm not really sure what that type is—but you're it."

"Really?" Mrs. Russo asked, gazing in her husband's direction. "Well, it doesn't matter," she said, shaking her head. "I've already made plans."

Just then, Max spotted a man walking up to them. Max recognized him as the activities director from the pool.

"All set," he told Mrs. Russo with a wink. "The boat's ready for us."

Max frowned. "*That* boat?" he asked.

The activities director looked across the dock. The small sailboat bobbing in the water was *sinking*!

As the man took off running, Mrs. Russo gave Max a suspicious look.

Max simply shrugged. He wasn't going to confess that he used magic to make the boat sink!

Hours later, back in the jungle, twilight descended and night closed in. Since it was too dark to keep moving, Alex and Justin built a campsite.

Using palm fronds and branches, they made an area to sleep in. Then Justin started a fire, and Alex placed rocks around it to keep the flames at bay.

Gazing into the flickering firelight, Alex hugged her knees to her chest. "What if we don't get to the stone in time?" she whispered. "What if we can't save everyone?"

"Don't think about it." Justin's voice was firm. "We *will*."

Alex sighed. "How do you know?"

Justin playfully tapped his sister's shoulder. "Between the two of us, how could we not?"

Alex finally smiled, and Justin lay back on

his bed of palm fronds. He thought about the magic they'd used today and the fact that if, and when, they actually made it through the next forty-eight hours, he and Alex would still be destined to go head-to-head in the family wizard competition.

"'Only those whose intentions are pure,'" Justin said to himself, still haunted by the words from the map's starting point. He turned to Alex. "How come you could open the path today and I couldn't?"

"I don't know," Alex replied. "All I was thinking about was saving our family."

"I was thinking about that, too—and how great it would be if I was the one to do it." Justin sighed. "I guess there's my answer."

Alex could see that Justin was upset. As he rolled onto his side, she quietly told him, "You're a great wizard, Justin."

Justin snorted. "I know a bunch of spells," he said. "That doesn't make me a great wizard."

"That isn't why I think you're great," Alex said gently. "You're always there for me. No matter how many times I screw up—you always try and make it better."

"That doesn't make me great," said Justin. "That just makes me your brother."

"I know I don't say it very often," Alex continued, "but . . . thank you."

Justin looked at her for a long moment, not even sure how to respond. "You're welcome," he finally said.

"Good night," Alex said.

"'Night, Alex," Justin replied. But he couldn't fall asleep. For a long time after that, he studied the stars, wondering who really was the better wizard.

Hours later, dawn broke over the treetops, and Justin heard the loud *snap!* of a twig cracking underfoot. He listened harder. *Snap! Snap! Snap!* Someone was sneaking up to their campsite!

"Alex, wake up!" he called. "Something's out there."

Opening her eyes, Alex saw a male figure moving toward them through the trees!

*"Ahhhh!"* she screamed, jumping up and destroying their makeshift beds in the process.

Alex and Justin summoned their magic powers, and together they slammed the approaching stranger against a tree.

Then they heard the squawking parrot and realized *who* the stranger was: Archie along with Giselle.

"Oh, my gosh," Justin said, "we are so sorry."

Alex nodded. "We didn't know who it was and Justin was all—'Something's out there!' Plus, I'm not really good in the morning."

"But you made it, that's great," Justin told Archie. "We were afraid we'd have to do this by ourselves—"

"Look!" Alex interrupted. She pointed to a line of cliffs in the distance. "There they are!" she cried. "The white cliffs. That's where the stone is!"

Alex ran to get the map. "See!" She pointed at the parchment. "Here it is."

Justin turned the map around and Alex grinned. "And here it is again. We're so close."

Her brother nodded and grabbed his backpack. "Let's go."

Meanwhile, back at the resort, Max was in his hammock, just waking up. Another night on the beach had left his dark hair mussed and his clothes wrinkled. But Max didn't care. Time was *really* running out now!

"Hey!" he called when he spotted his father leaving the resort's restaurant. He ran up to him. "You have to help me!"

"What's wrong?" Mr. Russo asked.

"I can't remember anything before the first grade!" Max cried. "And my brother and sister never came back last night!"

"Why are you telling me?" asked Mr. Russo. "Why don't you tell your parents?"

"It's a long story," Max said. "And my brother and sister are trying to find the Stone of Dreams."

Mr. Russo tensed. "That's incredibly dangerous."

"It was kind of your idea!" Max reminded him.

"I wasn't serious," said Mr. Russo. "I didn't think they'd actually try and do it."

"Please," said Max. "You're the only person I know who can help me find them."

Mr. Russo nodded. "Come on," he said. "I've got that map in my room."

A few minutes later, Mr. Russo was spreading the map out on a picnic table. He and Max leaned over and studied it.

"The problem is," said Mr. Russo, "it doesn't tell you where to start."

"Is that a *treasure* map?" a woman's voice suddenly asked.

Max and his father turned to find Mrs. Russo standing behind them. She had a cup of coffee in her hand and a curious look on her face.

"A treasure map?" Mr. Russo said nervously. "Don't be ridiculous."

But Mrs. Russo pressed on. She pushed between the two to get a better look. "It *is* a treasure map!" she declared.

"But not one that works," Mr. Russo warned.

"That's because we're missing a part," Max blurted out. "Justin and my sister . . . what's-her-name, had something that goes in this corner." He pointed. "There was a picture of some old fort with this gargoyle thingie on it."

"Oh, I know where that is!" Mrs. Russo cried. "I saw it on my artifact tour yesterday. Do I get to come with you?"

"No," Mr. Russo firmly replied.

"Why?" Mrs. Russo smiled. "Afraid you'll have to spend a little time with me?"

Mr. Russo blushed. "It's just that we can't, uh—" He glanced at Max. "*Tell* her."

But there was no way Max was going to tell his mom she couldn't come along. "That'd be great!" he replied instead.

Mr. Russo frowned. He couldn't understand why Max would want a mortal to come along with them.

"Oh, this is going to be fun!" Mrs. Russo declared. She dug into her bag for her rental-car keys. "I'll drive."

# CHAPTER 10

A short time later, Max and his parents arrived at the beginning of the secret jungle trail. Max's mom led them to the gargoyle-shaped rock she'd seen on her artifact tour.

"The map says that the path will only reveal itself to the one whose intentions are pure," Mrs. Russo said. "What does that mean?"

Mr. Russo folded his arms across his chest. "It means it's probably time for you to go. Thanks for your help, but we've got it from here."

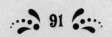

"There's no way I'm going now and letting you two have all the fun," his wife protested. "And"—she smiled slyly and waved the map—"neither of you reads Spanish, right?"

Max and his dad exchanged glances.

"Right," Mr. Russo admitted. "So I guess we'll have to figure this out together."

"The time for that is way over, people. Tick-tock!" Max cried.

Mr. Russo glanced down at the boy. "We can't just use . . . you know," he whispered referring to using magic in front of a mortal. "She'll *see*."

"Hey, lady, look over there!" Max shouted.

As Mrs. Russo glanced away, Max picked up the gargoyle-shaped rock and quickly focused his power. Reveal the path, he silently commanded. *Please!* My brother and sister need me!

Instantly, the tree branches parted, revealing the path. "Oh, wow!" Max exclaimed, pretending to be surprised. "There's a path! How could I have missed that? Come on!"

Mrs. Russo turned back around and frowned in confusion. "Where did that come from?" she wondered aloud.

As Max headed into the jungle with his parents, Alex and Justin found themselves at the entrance of a huge, dark cave.

Justin shuddered. They'd followed the map's directions out of the jungle and up to the line of white cliffs, and with the help of a little girl on a nearby farm, they'd finally found the cave that held the Stone of Dreams.

Justin could almost *feel* the stone's power emanating from the deep shadows ahead.

Just then, Archie lit a match. But a sudden puff of wind from inside the cave blew it out.

Justin frowned. He focused his power on the matchstick, but he couldn't relight it. "My magic's not working," he said. "The cave must be enchanted."

"My magic's not working either," Alex said. "But I really like that 'enchanted' excuse. I'm going to have to use that one."

Justin faced Archie and Giselle. "You two can wait here if you want."

Archie shook his head. "Not making that mistake again," he said. "We're in this togeth—"

Just then, Giselle dug her claws into Archie's shoulder. "Here is good," Archie said quickly. "Have I mentioned my fear of dark, scary places?"

Justin turned to his sister. "You ready?"

Alex peered into the chilly cave and swallowed. "No," she said. "But let's do it anyway."

Justin nodded. Then the two young wizards took a deep breath and moved forward. For a few minutes, they inched along in almost total darkness.

"Do we even know that this is the right cave?" Alex nervously asked her brother.

Suddenly, torches along the cave's walls lit up. Justin exchanged a look with his sister. "I'll go with *yes*," he said flatly, "but that's really just a hunch."

With the help of the torchlight, the two

could now make out a stone staircase carved into the cave wall in front of them. With a deep breath, they started up the steps.

"This *Piedra* thing better be able to reverse the spell," Alex said. "If not, I just got bat poo in my hair for nothing."

"It's the Stone of Dreams," Justin assured her. "It can do anything. Reverse any spell. Show you the future. But you only get one chance."

Moments later, the two young wizards were making their way down another torchlit passage. The walls were no longer rough stone. They looked polished and sleek, like museum marble.

This has to be man-made, Justin thought. Or *wizard*-made.

Suddenly, Alex stopped and said, "I'm sorry. For everything."

Justin turned around. "What?" he asked, stunned.

"I'm sorry," Alex repeated. "This is all my fault."

A smile spread across Justin's face. "I

know. I heard you the first time. I'm sorry, too," he said.

"Why are *you* sorry?" Alex asked him.

"That it took something like this for me to realize how much I need you," Justin told her sincerely.

Just then, the polished marble walls opened up into a huge craggy-walled cavern. Alex followed her brother into the enormous chamber—and gasped.

Stretching out before them was a field of sparkling pebbles. Red, gold, violet, orange, silver . . . a rainbow of colors shimmered in the torchlight.

"This is the place," Justin said in awe. "But how are we ever going to find the stone? It could be any one of these."

"Uh, I'm going with—*that* one!" Alex pointed. On the far side of the cavern a dazzling pink stone sat high up on a marble pedestal.

Justin's eyes widened. "Good guess."

Alex immediately moved to cross the field of pebbles and go to the stone. But Justin grabbed her arm and yanked her back.

"Watch out!" he cried.

Alex froze. The shimmering field of pebbles faded away. It was just an illusion. Peering down, she could now see that the center of the room was actually an open, bottomless pit!

She gulped. "Somebody should really put up a railing. Seriously, that's dangerous."

Justin pointed. There was only one way to get to the Stone of Dreams, as far as he could see: a narrow ledge running around the edge of the pit. At the far side of the cavern, steps led from it to the marble pedestal, which held the stone.

"I'll go," Justin said. He glanced at Alex, just to see if she had any other ideas before he went.

She didn't.

"I agree. *You* go," she said, looking at the pit nervously.

Justin nodded, and with his back to the wall, he began to inch his way along the ledge. He made it to the base of the stone steps—but as soon as he put his foot on the first one, it started to crumble.

"Be careful!" Alex cried.

But Justin didn't care about the risk. He *had* to keep going. This was the only way to the stone!

He took another step up. Then another and another. The steps continued to crumble behind him, but he was still making progress. The stone was so close now. He could almost reach it!

One more step, and—

"Ahhhh!" Justin yelled as the entire staircase finally gave way.

"Justin!" Alex shouted.

As the stone steps collapsed into the pit, Justin leaped for the ledge and just managed to catch it. With a grunt, he pulled himself back to safety.

"I'm okay!" he shouted to his sister. "Where's the stone?"

"I see it!" Alex cried, pointing.

When the stairs crumbled, so did the marble pedestal, sending the Stone of Dreams bouncing across the chasm and onto a rocky outcropping. Alex could see it just five feet below.

"I think I can reach it!" she called to her brother.

"Alex, no!" he warned. "It's too dangerous."

Alex could see her brother inching his way back around the ledge. But they had to get the stone as quickly as possible. And it was about time *she* stepped up and took a risk, too, she knew.

"I have to try," she called to Justin. And with a deep breath, she crawled down over the edge of the pit. She could *almost* reach the stone. All she had to do was hang on to a rock with one hand, lean out, and reach with the other—

"I got it!" She cheered.

Grinning with relief, she stared at the mirror-smooth rock. But before she could pull herself back to safety, her own foothold broke off. Suddenly, she was hanging by her fingertips. "Ahhh!" she cried.

"Alex!" Justin called above her.

"Help me," she croaked.

She tried to hold on, but her grip wasn't firm enough. Her fingers started slipping. She was going to fall into the bottomless pit below!

"Aahhhhh!" she cried once more.

*Smack!* Suddenly, a firm hand grabbed her wrist. She looked up. It was Justin.

"I won't let you fall," he told her as he began to pull her up.

As soon as she was back on solid ground, Alex hugged him gratefully.

"We got it," she told Justin. "We got the Stone. It's not too late to fix everything!"

But just as Alex held up the purple stone to show her brother, a horrible squawking noise filled the cavern. Before Alex knew what was happening, Giselle swooped in and, with her sharp parrot claws, snatched the stone right out of her hand!

"No!" Alex shouted. "What are you doing? Come back!"

# CHAPTER 11

No sooner had Giselle flown out of the chamber than Alex saw her father, mother, and brother walking in.

"Did you get it?" Max asked, running up to her and Justin.

"Is everybody okay?" Mr. Russo called.

"Dad!" Justin cried.

"Mom!" Alex shouted. She was *so* happy to see her! She threw her arms around her mother and hugged her tightly. "I am so sorry! You were right. I was wrong. I'll even repeat it if you want me to. I can't do this on my own. I need your help. I need you."

Still hugging her mom, Alex glanced down at Max. "How did you reverse the spell?" she asked him.

"I didn't," Max replied.

"Seriously," said Mrs. Russo, "what is with all this hugging?"

That's when Alex realized that her mom wasn't hugging her back. She let go. "You still don't know who I am, do you?" she asked her.

"No, I'm sorry—oh, wait!" said Mrs. Russo. "I do know you. You work at the resort."

She truly didn't have a clue, but Mr. Russo was beginning to understand.

"The other night at the pool," he said, "when you asked about reversing that spell. . . Who *are* you?" he asked the three kids.

"Hey, Dad," said Justin shyly.

"'*Dad*'? You didn't tell me you were married!" Mrs. Russo exclaimed. She threw up her hands. "Would somebody *please* explain to me what's going on?"

And so the kids did—or tried to, at least—as they made their way back through the jungle. By the time they were done, they'd almost reached the trail's starting point.

"No. This is ridiculous," Mrs. Russo said as they reached the clearing. "Would you listen to yourselves? Three kids show up and say we're their *parents*. It doesn't make any sense. I think I'd remember."

"No offense," Justin replied, "but if you remembered, we wouldn't be having this problem."

"And we're supposedly married!" Mrs. Russo went on, pointing to Mr. Russo. "We are *not* married."

"She's right." Mr. Russo nodded. "I mean I swore I would never . . ." His voice trailed off.

"Never *what*?" Mrs. Russo pressed.

Mr. Russo stopped walking. The path had ended. They were back at the beginning now. The crumbling stone marker was still there. The rental car was parked a few yards away.

With a deep breath, Mr. Russo turned to

his wife. "I swore I would never let myself fall in love with a mortal."

"And now?" Mrs. Russo asked.

"And now . . ." Mr. Russo held his wife's gaze. "Just tell me you're not falling for me and we'll know this isn't real."

Mrs. Russo blushed. "I can't tell you that."

Max couldn't take this drawn-out lovey-dovey stuff another second. "Look!" he cried. "Kiss. Don't kiss. I don't even have time to be squeamish about it. We've got to do something!"

"He's right." Mr. Russo turned toward Justin. "So how did you do the spell in the first place?"

"I did it." Alex stepped forward. "But I didn't mean to, I swear. Maybe right at the moment I meant it a little, but after that . . ." Sheepishly, she confessed, "I used your wand."

Mr. Russo took the silver wand out of his pocket. "This wand?"

Justin spoke up. "Can't you do something?"

Their dad took *The Book of Forbidden Spells*

out of his pocket and flipped through the pages. He read for a moment, then sadly shook his head. "No. I'm sorry. I can't. But it says that one of you might be able to reverse the spell." He glanced from Justin to Alex. "But only if you're a *full* wizard."

"The wizard competition is years away!" Max cried. "I have minutes, people!"

Max was right. As the youngest in the family, he was going to be the first to disappear. His memory was almost gone—he could barely remember his name anymore.

Justin turned to his sister. "The competition doesn't have to be years away."

Alex tensed up. "I'm not ready."

"I think you are," Justin told her. "We have to do this."

"How comes nobody ever considers *me* a threat?" Max grumbled.

Justin turned to his dad. "But you'd have to give up the wand. You'd have to believe absolutely that we're telling the truth."

"I know." Mr. Russo shifted nervously. "I can't go back on it."

Alex took his hand in hers. "You risked your life for us. Part of you has to know," she said.

Her dad turned to his wife. "If I don't do this," he explained, "they'll disappear forever."

"Mom, don't worry," Alex assured her. "It'll be okay."

But Mrs. Russo shook her head. It was all just too much for her to take in. "I'm sorry. I think you have the wrong woman," she said. "I would *not* forget my own kids. I've got to go." And with that, she headed for her rental car.

"Mom!" Alex cried, close to tears.

But Mrs. Russo didn't turn back around.

Justin put his arm around Alex, and Max moved closer, too.

"So is that lady your mom?" Max asked, looking confused.

Justin, Alex, and Mr. Russo all froze.

"Don't you remember who that is?" Alex asked her little brother.

Max scratched his head. "Should I?"

Mr. Russo faced his children. "We've got to do this now."

He held out the wand, and Justin and Alex both took hold of it. But just as Max reached out to grab it, too, a strange wind began to whip up around him.

*Oh, my gosh!* Alex thought. The space around Max rippled and swirled faster and faster, until a whirlpool formed, sucking Max into the middle!

"Max!" Justin called, grabbing for his brother's hand. But the rippling vortex was too powerful. A moment later, Max was gone.

"Max!" cried Mrs. Russo.

Sitting in her parked car, she'd watched the whole thing. She didn't understand any of this. But she was absolutely certain of *one* thing. Seeing that little boy disappear was like being punched in the heart.

"I do remember you," she said quietly.

*Max! Gone forever?* Alex didn't want to believe it. Then she heard her father's voice.

"Stay *focused*," he warned. "It's the only

way you can get him back. We've only got a few minutes before time catches up with you, too."

Alex and her brother put their hands back on the silver wand. Then Mr. Russo began to chant: *"A full wizard there can be but one. All power to a daughter or son. To ancient battle, transport us three. Where one shall emerge in victory."*

And in a burst of magical energy, all three of them suddenly vanished.

A moment later they found themselves in the middle of the old stone fort they'd visited on the first day of their vacation. Only now, strange banners flapped in the howling wind as ocean waves crashed against the ramparts. The castle was deserted, except for them.

Alex and Justin faced one another.

"Ready?" Mr. Russo asked.

"Wait!" Justin cried. "We don't even have wands!"

Mr. Russo tossed the silver wand into the air. It glistened in the sunlight, then shattered. Alex blinked as a piece of the wand magically appeared in her hand. She looked up to find Justin holding a piece of it as well.

"It's simple," Mr. Russo told them. "Whoever captures the power first will have it all."

As he spoke, Mr. Russo summoned all his magical energy into a single ball, which he held in his hands. The ball got larger and larger and began to pulse with light. Then he tossed it into the air, where it hovered over their heads.

"The loser will have nothing," Mr. Russo warned. *"Understand?* And if you don't try, it won't count."

Alex and Justin nodded at each other. "We'll try our hardest," Justin vowed.

Then, suddenly, there was a loud *pop*, and Alex and Justin vanished! A moment later, they reappeared on opposite ends of the fort. The ball of energy glowed above them, and they heard their father's voice. "The rules are simple. The only spells you're allowed to use are those involving the four elements. Earth, air, fire, and water."

"What?" Justin cried. "Nobody said that? I've been studying *battle* spells for the last ten years!"

"The best wizards can make the most out of the least," Mr. Russo said.

"Good," said Alex, "because that's pretty much all I've got."

"Wands at the ready," Mr. Russo commanded. "Ready . . . set . . . *magic!*"

# CHAPTER 12

The ball of energy dropped on the ground between the two young wizards, and both Justin and Alex ran toward it. Before Alex could reach the ball, however, she was cut off by a wall of flames.

"Justin!" she cried. Then she struck back with her own magic, turning the ground in front of her brother into quicksand with her wand.

*Splat!* Justin went in headfirst and came up sputtering. Alex, meanwhile, pointed her wand again and doused the fire with a fountain of water.

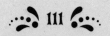

Then Justin turned the quicksand around him into dust. He waved his wand again, and suddenly Alex was stuck under a stormy rain cloud.

"Was the lightning really necessary?" she asked, her hair standing on end.

"Sorry!" Justin called. "But you know how unpredictable storms can be." Then he leaped for the ball of energy again. But he slipped on another patch of quicksand and landed on his face in the mud.

"Quit doing that!" Justin cried as the ball bounced away.

"Sorry," said Alex. "I just don't know a lot of spells!" She sprinted toward the ball. I have to do this, Alex thought. I just have to! I got my family into this, and it's up to me to get them out.

By now, Mrs. Russo had driven back to the resort. Her mind was racing. She didn't understand any of this, but for some reason, she desperately wanted to help that man, Jerry, and those children.

When she spotted Archie the magician by the resort's swimming pool, she crept closer. She knew that odd man had *something* to do with all this.

She could also see that he was arguing with a beautiful woman dressed in red, wearing a bright pink stone around her neck.

"But we did all of this for us," Archie was telling the woman. "So we could finally be together."

The woman tossed her silky hair to the side. "Oh, is that what you thought?"

"That's what you *said*," Archie cried.

"I was lying," the woman replied.

Mrs. Russo looked more closely at the stone around the woman's neck. *That's it!* Mrs. Russo realized. The Stone of Dreams! She rushed up to the pair.

"*You!*" she said to the woman. "*You* were that *bird*!"

"I don't know what you're talking about," Giselle said, pausing to cough up a bright blue feather.

"Yesterday, that would have freaked me

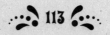

out," said Mrs. Russo. "But now . . . I need that stone."

"I don't think so," Giselle replied snippily.

"Look," Mrs. Russo went on, almost in tears, "I don't know what's going on. I'm not part of your world. But I do know that I just got my heart ripped out by a boy who I didn't even know I knew, let alone loved . . . and his father, who may or may not be my husband—but I think I'd like him to be— and two other wonderful kids . . . It's a little confusing. They need that stone." She paused and glared at Giselle. "And I'm getting it one way or another."

But Giselle just grinned and, without blinking, magically slammed Mrs. Russo up against a wall. "Then it's going to be 'or another,'" she said coolly. "I'm not letting those kids turn me in to the authorities. I just got my life back. Why don't you consider this a fresh start? From what I saw, it didn't look like you and your daughter got along so well. Believe me, there are a lot of moms who'd like to be in your position."

"Give me that stone," Mrs. Russo demanded.

"You mean *this* one?" asked Archie, suddenly stepping up beside her. He held out the purple stone. He had magically taken it from Giselle.

Giselle stared at him in disbelief. "What are you doing?" she demanded.

"It's the first trick in my new act," he told her. "It's a real doozy."

Giselle suddenly coughed up a few more feathers. "What did you—" she began. But before she could finish, there was a flash of light. When it subsided, the woman was gone, and Giselle was back in parrot form.

"Turns out, I like you better as a bird," Archie said, setting the parrot on his shoulder. He gave the stone to Mrs. Russo.

"Thank you," Mrs. Russo told him. She held on to the stone tightly. Now she just hoped she hadn't run out of time!

Meanwhile, among the ruins of the ancient fort, Alex was running toward the ball of magical energy. Suddenly, she felt as if she

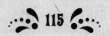

were wading through water. She looked down to find that she was literally melting!

She heard her brother laugh. "A little variation on your puddle spell," he said. Then Justin raced toward the glowing ball. Alex tried to follow, but she couldn't free her legs.

"Sorry," Justin said. "But we have to end this."

Alex kept struggling. But there was nothing she could do. Then she suddenly noticed a tiny flower growing between two big rocks.

That's it! she realized. Earth, air, sun, and water. That's all you need. And she began to chant: *"Elements of earth unite. It's time to win this fight. Earth, air, sun, and water, combine all four to grow a daughter!"*

The next moment, she vanished!

Where did Alex go? Justin wondered.

A second later, Alex popped out of the ground right beneath the glowing ball. She sprouted up like a flower, unfolding and blooming as she grew, and reached out her arms. Before Justin could stop her, Alex grasped the ball of mystical energy. A giant explosion knocked Justin to the ground, and in the center of the blast, Alex began to glow.

"I did it!" Alex cried. "I won!"

"Congratulations," Justin said, standing up and dusting himself off.

But Alex didn't have much time to celebrate before Mr. Russo came running up to them.

"Hurry!" he told her. "You haven't got much time!"

"Oh, right. Okay," said Alex. Then she froze. "But I don't know what to do! Justin, help me!" she begged. "What spell do I use?"

"Why would I help you?" asked Justin.

"Because you're my brother," said Alex. "I'm sorry you didn't win, but—"

"I'm your *brother*?" said Justin. He stared at her blankly.

Alex and her dad shared a panicked look.

"Oh, no. Justin . . ." Alex gasped. Now *he* was beginning to forget his past. "I can't do it without you. Please. Remember. I'm your little sister. I taunt you and tease you and make your life miserable, but you love me anyway. You're everything I ever want to be, and I'm totally jealous of how smart you are and how nice and honest and kind. I know I should have told you that before. . . . Justin, you can't leave me alone. Please!"

"I'd never leave you," he replied. "I don't remember you, but I believe you."

Alex hugged him tightly. "Okay, what's the spell?" she asked him.

He took a breath. "It's complicated, but—"

Suddenly, before he could say any more, Justin's body began to flicker. The space around him began to ripple and swirl.

"No! Justin!" Alex cried.

But it was too late. The same vortex that had taken Max appeared and whisked Justin away, as well.

With tears in her eyes, Alex turned to her father. "What do I do? Justin should have won this, not me."

"Be calm," Mr. Russo told her. "You can do it."

Alex wiped the tears from her eyes—and then she closed them.

Concentrating intently, she remembered

her family and her life as it once was. More than anything, she wanted it back. With all her heart and soul, she chanted: *"Reverse the spell. Don't make me scream and yell. Because of words of hate, do not my brother take!"*

Then Alex waited. But nothing happened.

She whirled around to face her dad. *"Please.* You *have* to help."

But Mr. Russo shook his head. "I'm sorry. I think it's too late."

*"No!"* Alex cried. "It *can't* be too late!"

"Hey!" a voice called from the rampart above them.

Alex looked up to see her mother peering down at them.

"Would this help?" Mrs. Russo called, tossing the Stone of Dreams to Alex.

"The stone . . . ?" gasped Alex.

"Be careful," Mr. Russo warned. "You only get the *one* wish. If you do it right, you can get your brothers back and still be a full wizard. Just wish for them all to reappear."

Alex looked at her glowing palms. "But . . ." she began. Then she shook her head. "No, it's

···· 119 ·····

more than that," she told her parents. And with that, she closed her eyes and clenched the shimmering stone tightly in her fist. "I want everything to be *exactly* the way it was."

When Alex opened her eyes, she was back in her hotel room. The silver wand and *The Book of Forbidden Spells* were in her hands.

"Alex?" Mrs. Russo called.

"Mom?" she said. She spun around and saw her mother in the doorway.

"The minute Justin tried to magically glue me to my chair, I knew something was up," said Mrs. Russo. "You just will not stop, will you?"

"Mom!" Alex cried, dropping the wand and spell book and throwing her arms around her mother. "I am so sorry," she cried. "I could never hate you. I love you. You know that, right? And I'm not just saying it. I really mean it."

"Of course I know that," said Mrs. Russo. She looked at Alex in confusion. "But you're still grounded."

"Yes, I know," said Alex, beaming. "I can't wait to be grounded. Ground me. Take away my magic. I don't care."

Still confused, Mrs. Russo scratched her head. "Well, as long as you've learned your lesson."

"Alex?!" Just then, Justin and Max called her name from outside the room.

"Justin! Max!" Alex exclaimed, running out to meet them.

"You miss your *brothers*?" asked Mrs. Russo, now *truly* bewildered.

Alex rushed up to Justin and Max and gave them each a big hug.

"What did you do?" Justin asked.

Alex held up her hands. Their magical glow was gone, along with all the power she had won in the competition. Justin looked at the magic fading from her hands in awe.

"You gave it up? But you won! Why would you do that?" asked Justin.

"Because I wanted to make sure that nothing was different . . . that nothing changed," Alex explained.

"You know, this just means that the next time, I'm winning," Justin said with a smile.

Alex smirked. "Oh, no. I'll still beat you."

"People. I'm right here," Max reminded them.

"Yes, you are, and I love you for that," Alex said, hugging him again.

*Everything* had gone back to the way it was—*exactly* the way it was—including their wizard-in-training status.

Just then, Mr. Russo walked up. "What's going on?" he asked.

Mrs. Russo joined them. "Hugging. I'm not quite sure why," she answered with a shrug.

"Dad!" Alex cried, running up to hug him.

"A *lot* of hugging," Mrs. Russo went on.

"Excuse me, Alex . . ." a boy's voice said to her.

Alex turned to find Javier in the doorway.

"Alex, honey," her mother said. "If you want to go to the party for an hour, I'd be okay with that."

Alex blinked. "Well, *I* wouldn't be," she

told her mom. Then she turned to Javier. "Go bother somebody who doesn't have their mom watching out for them. Bye-bye, now," she said with a wave. Javier frowned and slunk away. Then Alex turned back to her mother.

"Oh, hey, we should get a picture," she said, noticing her mother's camera. She took it from her mom. "I'll set it up."

But Mrs. Russo stopped her. "That's okay. I think we have enough pictures," she said. "Besides, I'll definitely remember this moment without one." She put her arm around Alex and kissed her warmly on the top of her head. Then, all five Russos headed to the beach to enjoy the rest of their family vacation.